# DORLING KINDERSLEY *READERS*  LEGO

# Secret at Dolphin Bay

Written by Marie Birkinshaw • Illustrated by Jason Cook

BEGINNING **1** TO READ

A Dorling Kindersley Book

Fay Fixit and Steve Spanner
were busy mending
Lifeguard Sally's truck.

# A Note to Parents and Teachers

The *Dorling Kindersley Readers* series is a reading programme for children, which is highly respected by teachers and educators around the world. The LEGO Group has a global reputation for offering high quality, innovative products, specially designed to stimulate a child's creativity and development through play.

Now Dorling Kindersley has joined forces with the LEGO Group, to produce the first-ever graded reading scheme to be based around LEGO play themes. Each *Dorling Kindersley Reader* is guaranteed to capture a child's imagination, whilst developing his or her reading skills, general knowledge and love of reading.

The books are written and designed in conjunction with literacy experts, including Cliff Moon M Ed, Honorary Fellow of the University of Reading.

Cliff Moon spent many years as a teacher and teacher educator, specializing in reading. He has written more than 140 books for children and teachers, and he reviews regularly for teachers' journals.

The four levels of *Dorling Kindersley Readers* are aimed at different reading abilities, enabling you to choose the books that are right for each child.

**Level 1** – Beginning to Read
**Level 2** – Beginning to Read Alone
**Level 3** – Reading Alone
**Level 4** – Proficient Readers

The 'normal' age at which a child begins to read can be anywhere from three to eight years old, so these levels are only guidelines.

Dorling DK Kindersley

LONDON, NEW YORK, SYDNEY, DELHI, PARIS,
MUNICH and JOHANNESBURG

**Senior Editor** Cynthia O'Neill
**Senior Art Editor** Nick Avery
**Senior Managing Art Editor**
Cathy Tincknell
**DTP Designer** Andrew O'Brien
**Production** Nicola Torode

**Reading Consultant**
Cliff Moon M.Ed.

First published in Great Britain in 2000 by
Dorling Kindersley Limited
9 Henrietta Street
Covent Garden, London WC2E 8PS

2 4 6 8 10 9 7 5 3 1

www.LEGO.com

A CIP catalogue record for this book is available
from the British Library.

ISBN 0-7513-2867-7

Colour reproduction by Dot Gradations, UK
Printed and bound by L Rex, China

see our complete
catalogue at
**www.dk.com**

Steve tested the brakes and
Fay put some oil in the engine.

"Thanks for your help!"
said Sally.

"Now I must get back to work.
This afternoon, we're testing
the new rescue boat."

"Can we come with you?"
asked Steve.
"We aren't very busy today,"
Fay told Sally.

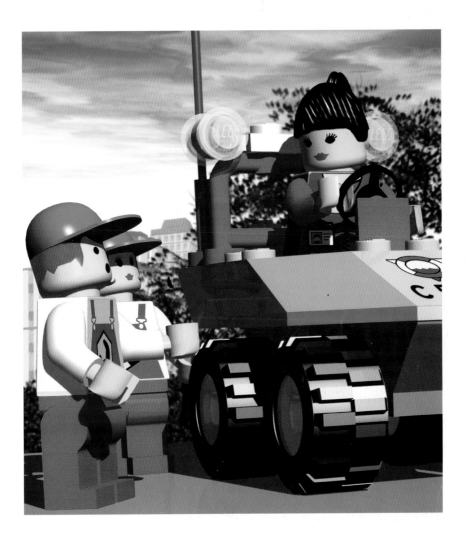

At the harbour,
Steve and Fay helped Diver Dan
push the boat onto the water.

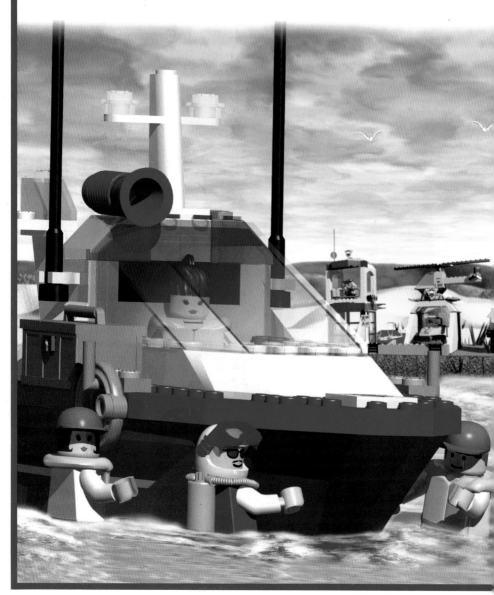

Then the friends climbed
on board the boat.
"Let's go!" said Sally.

On the boat deck
was a box of new tools.
"I wish we could test these tools!"
Steve joked to Fay.

Suddenly, the alarm sounded.

# Eee-ohh! Eee-ohh!

Sally called back to base and talked to the coast guards. Then she spoke to her friends. "A dinghy is in trouble," she said. "We must go to Dolphin Bay!"

At Dolphin Bay,
Tessa the sea vet
was waiting for help.

"I came to help a dolphin
who had cut his flipper,"
said Tessa.
"But now my boat won't start!"

"Don't worry," Fay told Tessa.
"We've been looking forward
to testing the new tools!"

"We'll be busy too,"
Lifeguard Sally said to Dan.
"We must find out
how the dolphin cut his flipper."

"I think there's some sharp metal
hidden under the water,"
said Tessa.
"I'll try to find it
with the underwater camera,"
Sally told her.

"I'll dive down and look too," said Diver Dan.

19

Dan jumped into the sea.
Some rainbow fish followed him
as he swam about,
looking for the sharp metal.

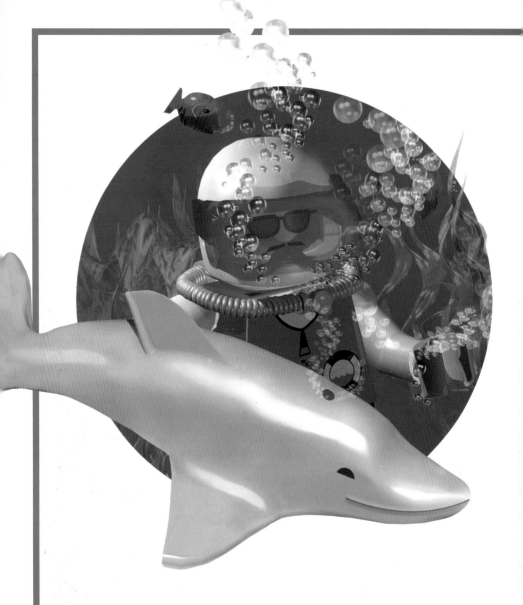

Then the dolphin swam up to Dan.
He tapped Dan's arm
with his nose!
Then he swam away.

"Maybe the dolphin
wants me to follow him,"
thought Dan.
So he swam after the dolphin.

Fay and Steve had mended
Tessa's boat.
"Thank you so much,"
said Tessa.

Then Diver Dan
came back to the surface.
"The dolphin has led me
to a metal box," he said.
"It has very sharp sides.
Let's pull it out of the sea."

Everyone helped to pull
the metal box from the sea.
It was very heavy.

Dan opened the box carefully.
What a surprise!
The box was full of treasure!
"I wonder if this is stolen?"
said Sally.

Back at LEGO City harbour,
the police were waiting.

They looked at the treasure.
"This is gold from the castle,"
they said.
"A robber stole it long ago and
now we can take it back."

But when the harbour police
tried to leave,
their boat wouldn't start.

"Let's get to work!"
Steve said to Fay.
"Time to test those tools again!"

# What do they do?

## Mechanics

fix broken-down machines.

## Lifeguards

help keep swimmers and sailors safe.

## Harbour police

keep law and order out at sea.

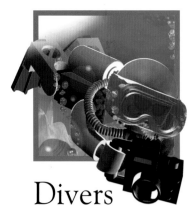

## Divers

swim underwater and explore the sea.